No Hugs!

To Avie and Maddy, I love you!—D.A.P.
For Tom, who gives the best hugs.—S.J.

Text copyright © 2019 Deirdre A. Prischmann • Illustrations copyright © 2019 Sarah Jennings

Published in 2019 by Amicus Ink, an imprint of Amicus • P.O. Box 1329 • Mankato, MN 56002 • www.amicuspublishing.us

Library of Congress Cataloging-in-Publication Data
Names: Prischmann, Deirdre A., author. | Jennings, Sarah, illustrator.
Title: No hugs! / by Deirdre A. Prischmann ; illustrated by Sarah Jennings.
Description: Mankato, MN : Amicus Ink, [2019] | Summary: Alice loves giving hugs and does not understand
why her friend Zara does not want one, until the tables are turned, giving her a new perspective.
Identifiers: LCCN 2018048698 (print) | LCCN 2018052965 (ebook) | ISBN 9781681525198 (ebook) | ISBN 9781681524153 (hardcover)
Subjects: | CYAC: Hugging—Fiction. | Friendship—Fiction.
Classification: LCC PZ7.1.P768 (ebook) | LCC PZ7.1.P768 No 2019 (print) | DDC [E]—dc23
LC record available at https://lccn.loc.gov/2018048698

Editor: Rebecca Glaser
Designer: Kathleen Petelinsek

First edition 9 8 7 6 5 4 3 2 1 • Printed in China

No Hugs!

by Deirdre A. Prischmann

illustrated by Sarah Jennings

amicus ink

Mankato, Minnesota